The Increased Difficulty of Concentration

A Play in Two Acts

by Vaclav Havel

Translated from the Czech by
Vera Blackwell

A SAMUEL FRENCH ACTING EDITION

SAMUEL FRENCH

FOUNDED 1830

New York Hollywood London Toronto

SAMUELFRENCH.COM

ISBN 978-0-573-61082-0   Printed in U.S.A.   #11048

MUSIC USE NOTE

**IMPORTANT BILLING AND CREDIT
REQUIREMENTS**

LIST OF CHARACTERS

DR. EDUARD HUML, *social scientist*

VLASTA HUML, *his wife*

RENATA, *his mistress*

BLANKA, *his secretary*

DR. ANNA BALCAR, *social scientist*

KAREL KRIEBL, *technician*

EMIL MACHAL, *surveyor*

MR. BECK, *supervisor*

The Increased Difficulty of Concentration

ACT ONE

HUML'S *Flat: A cross between a living-room and a hall. A small staircase Left leading up to the bedroom [upstairs room:* U. D.*]. There are three doors downstairs: left door [*L. D.*] leading to the study; back door [*B. D.*] to the kitchen, the bathroom and all other parts of the flat; right door [*R. D.*], equipped with a peephole, is the main entrance. Upstage, a mirror and a commode with a cactus on it. Downstage, a dining table with four chair around it. Throughout, the audience should be prevented from distinguishing the objects currently displayed on the table; their view can be partially obscured by a flower-stand, for example. At Right, an easy-chair flanked by a small table with telephone.*

For a moment the Stage is empty, B. D. *is open; then* MRS. HUML, *wearing a dressing-gown over her dress, enters by* B. D. *She carries a tray with breakfast for two: cups, saucers, tea-pot, rolls, butter. Setting the table, she calls towards the bedroom.*

MRS. HUML. Breakfast! (*When she has finished the table,* MRS. HUML *pours the tea, sits down and begins to eat, while* U. D. *opens and* HUML *enters in his pajamas, dishevelled, obviously just out of bed, leisurely descends, sits down opposite* MRS. HUML, *spreads a napkin in his lap and also starts eating. Longish silence is finally interrupted by* MRS. HUML.) Well?

HUML. Have we some honey?

MRS. HUML. Failed again, I bet.

HUML. Couldn't help it.

MRS. HUML. Why?

HUML. The atmosphere wasn't right.

MRS. HUML. Where did you go?

HUML. Flics. Cartoons.

MRS. HUML. What an idea! And then?

HUML. She went on telling funny stories and jokes, it just didn't seem right. Have we some honey?

MRS. HUML. And you couldn't steer the conversation to more serious subjects, I suppose.

HUML. I tried. But every time she'd cut in with some new story. She was full of fun and games, that's all. Nothing I could do about it. Have we some honey?

MRS. HUML. In the cupboard. (HUML *puts down his napkin, gets up and shuffles out by* B. D., *leaving it open. Pause.*)

HUML. (*Offstage.*) Can't find it—

MRS. HUML. (*Calling toward* B. D.) On the top shelf— (*Longish pause.*)

HUML. (*Offstage.*) Where?

MRS. HUML. Oh, for heaven's sake! (*Jumps up, runs out by* B. D. *Offstage.*) And what's this? (*Shortly after,* L. D. *slowly opens and* HUML *quietly backs in, apparently hoping his exit from the study will not be noticed. He is fully dressed and spruced up. Carefully, he pushes the door almost shut, then quickly tiptoes to* B. D. *and calls softly through it.*)

HUML. Come! (RENATA, *wearing a coat, appears in the door.* HUML *grabs her hand and leads her swiftly towards* R. D., *looks around stealthily, then kisses* RENATA'S *cheek. Whispers.*) Bye, kitty-cat.

RENATA. (*Whispers.*) Bye. And don't you forget!

(HUML *peers through the peephole, then quietly opens the door and lets* RENATA *out; quickly closes door, runs back, closes* B. D., *after which he ambles to*

L. D., *quietly opens it and holds it open. Presently, MISS BALCAR and KRIEBL enter, wearing lab-coats, carefully carrying Puzuk between them. Puzuk is a complicated piece of machinery, faintly reminiscent of a cash register and/or a calculator. It is furnished with a keyboard, various push-buttons, a small crank on one side, an eyepiece not unlike that of a microscope, a red and a green bulb, a small loudspeaker, and a long cord with a plug. MISS BALCAR and KRIEBL place Puzuk gently on the table, HUML closes L. D.*)

KRIEBL. (*To* HUML.) Where's the socket?

HUML. There—behind the cactus. (KRIEBL *crosses to back wall, trailing the cord, sticks plug into socket. MISS BALCAR sits down in the easy-chair. KRIEBL returns, sits at Puzuk and begins to fiddle with its machinery. HUML also sits down, examining the apparatus with some curiosity.*) So that's what he's like!

MISS BALCAR. Nice, isn't he?

HUML. Nice. May I ask how he works?

MISS BALCAR. Well, we fed him with some basic information about you which had been placed at our disposal, he processed it, and on the basis of it he's now going to ask you his first question. You're going to give him an honest answer, he'll process your answer—together with other data concerning your environment, researched for him by Mr. Machal—after which he'll proceed with his next question to you. He'll go on in this way until the sum total of the received information forms a coherent pattern inside him.

HUML. How interesting! He sort of does your work for you, doesn't he?

MISS BALCAR. At a certain stage—

HUML. That's what I mean—at a certain stage— (KRIEBL *is still fiddling with Puzuk, worrying the keyboard, turning the crank, peering into the eyepiece, etc. MISS BALCAR stares at him.*)

Miss Balcar. Anything wrong, Mr. Kriebl?

Kriebl. He felt rather cool, so Machal and I massaged his control panel a bit to warm him up to the right degree.

Miss Balcar. And what about the electrodes?

Kriebl. Functioning. We can start—

Miss Balcar. Splendid! Now, put down— (*Dictating.*) Eduard Huml, 1928—beginning of interview 15:25—first question. (*Calls.*) Silence, please!

(Kriebl, *having typed the data on the keyboard, turns the crank, peers into the eyepiece, and presses a button. The loudspeaker gives out a soft rumbling. Kriebl stares closely at his watch; general suspense. Suddenly, the* U. D. *opens and* Machal *appears, wearing a lab-coat, with a pencil stuck behind his ear.* Kriebl *again quickly presses a button and turns the crank. The rumbling stops.* Machal *takes no notice of anybody, slowly descends, halts, counts the steps, produces from his pocket a grubby slip of paper on which he notes the ascertained number. Having finished, he slowly crosses to* Kriebl *and hands him the slip of paper.*)

Kriebl. Thanks, Emil— (Kriebl *smooths out the slip of paper on the table, then slides it into Puzuk.* Machal *ambles out by* L. D.)

Miss Balcar. Ready now?

Kriebl. Ready.

Miss Balcar. (*Calls.*) Silence, please! (Kriebl *again turns the crank, presses a button, Puzuk begins to rumble. Once more,* Kriebl *stares closely at his watch; general suspense. After a while, Puzuk's red light goes on.*) Red! (Kriebl *quickly presses a button and turns the crank. The light goes out and the rumbling stops. Awkward pause.*) He's overheated. You must have massaged him too hard—

KRIEBL. We massaged him just right; more likely it's a stuck switch.

MISS BALCAR. What shall we do?

KRIEBL. He must cool off a bit. (*To* HUML.) Have you a fridge?

HUML. Yes. In the kitchen— (KRIEBL *unplugs Puzuk's cord and together with* MISS BALCAR *carries Puzuk out by* B. D. *which has meanwhile been opened by* HUML. HUML *follows, leaving door open. Pause. Offstage.*) Will he get in?

KRIEBL. (*Offstage.*) Do you mind if I take out the milk bottles for a moment?

HUML. (*Offstage.*) Not in the least— (*Shortly after, they all return by* B. D., *slowly cross to the table, sit down as before and wait. Longish uneasy pause.*)

MISS BALCAR. Hope he won't get too cold in there—

KRIEBL. He'll make himself heard when he's cold!

MISS BALCAR. Let's hope so— (*Longish uneasy pause.*)

KRIEBL. (*To* HUML.) Fond of fruit?

HUML. How did you know?

KRIEBL. I saw your supplies in the kitchen—

HUML. My mother lives in the country, so she sends us some occasionally—

KRIEBL. Good for you— (*Longish uneasy pause.*)

MISS BALCAR. (*To* KRIEBL.) What about giving him an electric shock?

KRIEBL. Better not. That usually gives him stray thoughts. And also the condensor is likely to get troublesome then— (*Longish uneasy pause. To* HUML). You come from the country?

HUML. Yes.

KRIEBL. Mountains?

HUML. How did you know?

KRIEBL. The plums your mother sent you grow only in high altitudes.

HUML. Yes, they are indeed high altitude plums. (*Longish uneasy pause.*)

MISS BALCAR. (*To* KRIEBL.) When did you oil him last?

KRIEBL. Day before yesterday.

MISS BALCAR. Day before yesterday?

KRIEBL. That's right.

MISS BALCAR. So that in fact he's been freshly oiled—

KRIEBL. Right. (*Longish uneasy pause.*)

HUML. (*To* MISS BALCAR.) May I ask you something?

MISS BALCAR. By all means—

HUML. The questions I'm going to be asked by the instrument—

MISS BALCAR. Puzuk—

HUML. I mean Puzuk—have they a specific investigational objective?

MISS BALCAR. What do you mean?

HUML. I'd be interested to know whether this is a matter of a specific case to which my testimony is somehow related, or just a sort of—how shall I put it—complex investigation—sort of preventive evidence—

MISS BALCAR. Why the alternatives? Our investigation is complex precisely because it is concerned with a specific case.

HUML. Oh! I see! And can you tell me who is your subject?

MISS BALCAR. Who? You, of course.

HUML. Me? (*Just then, Puzuk's sharp siren starts wailing Offstage.*)

KRIEBL. What did I tell you! Now he's cold!

(MISS BALCAR *and* KRIEBL *jump up and run out by* B. D., *leaving it open,* HUML *starts to follow. Before he gets to the door,* RENATA *enters by* B. D., *wearing* MRS. HUML'S *apron, and carefully carrying a tray with lunch: two plates with steaming stew, a pot of mustard, a basket with bread, glasses, beer, knives and forks. She begins setting the table.* HUML *crosses to table and helps* RENATA. *Then they both sit down and start eating. Longish pause, finally interrupted by* RENATA.)

RENATA. You're not just trying to jolly me along, are you?

HUML. Not in the least. I want to put an end to it, I really do. Only you've got to try and understand it's not an easy matter. We've lived together for ten years, she has nobody but me, she can't imagine her life without me—some beer?

RENATA. Just a drop— (HUML *pours beer for* RENATA *and himself, then continues.*)

HUML. Prospectively, she rather counts on my parting with you and living again only with her—well, you know how it is, women are terribly sensitive about these things; in any case, it's going to be a blow for her.

RENATA. I've never even suggested you shouldn't do it tactfully, that goes without saying, doesn't it? (*Pause. They go on eating.*)

HUML. Why don't you take some mustard—

RENATA. Sorry, I loathe mustard— (*Pause. They go on eating.*) Listen, Eddi—

HUML. Yes?

RENATA. Glad I've come?

HUML. You know I am—

RENATA. Why don't you say something tender to me?

HUML. You know my imagination doesn't work that way—

RENATA. A man who's in love always finds a way to express what he feels!

HUML. I think you're attractive—

RENATA. That's not much, is it?

HUML. I'm very fond of you—

RENATA. Is that all?

HUML. Sorry, kitty-cat, I'm really no good at using

big words! Which doesn't mean, however, that I don't
feel anything—

RENATA. If you felt something big, no words would
seem big enough to you! (*Excitedly.*) After all, we can
part, just say the word!

HUML. Starting that again, are you!

RENATA. I'm a fool, I really am! (RENATA *throws
down her knife and fork, jumps up in great agitation,
runs out sobbing by* L. D. *and slams it.* HUML *finishes
his bite, gets up, crosses to* L. D., *tries the door; it is
locked. He hesitates, then addresses the locked door.*)

HUML. Renata— (*Pause.*) Kitty-cat— (*Pause.*)
Come on! (*Pause.*) Remember the Dolomites! In that
old kiln? (*He waits a while. As there is no response
from* RENATA, *he shrugs and walks back. Just then,*
BLANKA *enters by* R. D., *closes the door, crosses to the
table, sits down, takes shorthand pad and pencil and
gets ready for dictation.*) Where did we stop?

BLANKA. (*Reads.*) Various people have at various
times and in various circumstances various needs—

HUML. Ah! Yes— (*Begins to pace thoughtfully to
and fro, while dictating to* BLANKA, *who takes it down
in shorthand.*) and thus attach to various things
various values—full stop. Therefore, it would be mistaken to set up a fixed scale of values, valid for all
people in all circumstances and at all times—full stop.
This does not mean, however, that in all of history
there exist no values common to the whole of man-
kind—full stop. If those values did not exist, man-
kind would not form a unified whole—full stop. Yet,
as a rule, each man—each period—each social group
—has its own scale of values, by which the basic,
universal values are in a certain way made more con-
crete—full stop. At the same time, an individual scale
of values is always somehow related to other—more
general—scales of values—for instance, to those belonging to a given period—which form a sort of frame-

work, or background, to the individual scales—full
stop. Would you mind reading me the last sentence?
BLANKA. (*Reads.*) At the same time, an individual
scale of values is always somehow related to other,
more general, scales of values, for instance, to those
belonging to a given period, which form a sort of
framework, or background, to the individual scales.
HUML. That's pretty good. Let's go on. Among the
most basic values of present-day man one can include,
for example, work—in other words—the opportunity
to do that which would enable man to fulfil himself
completely, to develop his own specific potentialities,
his relationships with other people, his moral principles
—certain convictions regarding his concept of the
world, his faith in something to which he can commit
his life—full stop. Got it?
BLANKA. Yes.
HUML. Good. And now a new paragraph, please. The
state in which man finds himself after he has satisfied
one of his particular needs—i.e. when he has achieved
a particular value—is called happiness—full stop.
However, since—as we have already said—people
have— (*He stops, ponders, then turns to* BLANKA.)
Blanka—
BLANKA. Yes, Dr. Huml?
HUML. That Rudy of yours—is he your first love?
BLANKA. Yes.
HUML. How old is he?
BLANKA. Eighteen.
HUML. Eighteen? Really? (*Pause. He becomes
dreamy.*) Eighteen! When I was eighteen! Good God!
I was devouring Hegel, Schopenhauer, Nietzsche,
writing essays on metaphysics, editing a student mag-
azine, I was hopelessly in love with a medical student,
Ann Gluecksmann—by the way, you remind me of her
a little—and in addition, I still managed to frequent
the Pygmalion Bar daily and play football for the

Liberal Youth Club twice a week! What a strange time that was—rather nice— (*Pause.*) Where did we stop?

BLANKA. (*Reads.*) However, since, as we have already said, people have—

HUML. (*Again begins to pace thoughtfully to and fro while dictating.*) However, since—as we have already said—people have a great variety of needs and thus consider a great variety of things to be of value —the content of a state of happiness is also extremely varied—full stop. This is why, in spite of the fact that we all have our own precise image of what is happiness, we find it very hard to agree on a particular definition of happiness which would be satisfactory for all—full stop. New paragraph—

BLANKA. Excuse me a moment— (*Gets up and walks towards* B. D.)

HUML. Ah! The water's boiling! (BLANKA *exits by* B. D., HUML *follows, the door stays open. Pause.*)

MRS. HUML. (*Offstage.*) And what's this?

HUML. (*Offstage.*) There's honey in that?

(MRS. HUML *enters by* B. D., *wearing a dressing-gown over her dress, sits down at table and continues with her breakfast. Shortly after,* HUML *shuffles in by* B. D., *in his pajamas, dishevelled, carrying a jar of honey. He, too, sits down at table and goes on with his breakfast. To start with, he dabs honey on a roll. Pause.*)

MRS. HUML. Oh well, another opportunity missed!

HUML. Look, it's not the last time I'm going to see her—she's supposed to drop in today, I'll give it another try—

MRS. HUML. One time she's full of fun, next time you're sorry for her, another time you're not feeling well—listen, be honest, aren't you perhaps postponing the whole thing on purpose?

HUML. Why on earth should I do that?

MRS. HUML. Maybe you actually love her—

HUML. You know very well I don't love her! I only find her sexually exciting, and even that far less than at the beginning.

MRS. HUML. Let's hope so! And what do you say to her when she asks if you love her?

HUML. When possible, I try to change the subject. Want some?

MRS. HUML. Quite right! Would you put some on my roll?

HUML. (*Dabs honey on her roll.*) Of course, she got me up against the wall a few times, so I couldn't help giving her a positive answer.

MRS. HUML. But it didn't come from your heart, did it?

HUML. No. Here you are— (*Passes her the roll.*)

MRS. HUML. Listen, Eddi—

HUML. Mmnn—

MRS. HUML. Promise me you'll finally wind it up in some reasonable way. We just can't go on like this! It makes me suffer more than you think. Most of all in the evenings when I sit at home, mending your socks or your underpants—and all the time I know you're with her, having fun, spending our money, driving her about in our car, kissing her— (*Pause. They continue their breakfast.*) I'm sure you'll think I'm being silly, but do you know what bothers me most at those moments?

HUML. What?

MRS. HUML. The idea that you might just then be sleeping with her!

HUML. You know very well that I don't sleep with her so often; after all, we have nowhere to go. We usually end up by kissing; at the very most I might touch her breasts a bit. Pass me a roll, will you—

MRS. HUML. (*Passing him a roll.*) I hope you aren't making it all up just to calm me down! Does it ever occur to you what it's like for me, having to pretend in front of others that I don't know anything, to put up with their meaningful glances and ignore them, having to play the silly housewife who doesn't know what's going on! Besides, if it's not worth your while to break it off on my account, you ought to do it for your own sake—just look at yourself! Can't you see the way you're slipping? Do you read anything at all any more?

Huml. More butter?

Mrs. Huml. Finish it, if you like.

Huml. I told you, didn't I, I want to do it in stages—

Mrs. Huml. I know your blessed stages, so far you haven't budged!

Huml. What do you mean? Only last night I began to prepare the ground—

Mrs. Huml. Did you? How?

Huml. Well, to start with, I didn't kiss her neck as I usually do—

Mrs. Huml. You kiss her neck? You've never told me that!

Huml. She likes it and it excites me too in a way.

Mrs. Huml. And then? Did you tell her you still love me?

Huml. For a start, I said I like you as the companion of my life.

Mrs. Huml. Well, that's at least something. What did she say?

Huml. She insisted I should divorce you.

Mrs. Huml. I hope you didn't promise her any such thing!

Huml. She was so insistent, I had to agree—on the surface. But deep down I kept my own counsel and I didn't commit myself to anything definite. Listen, Vlasta, hate to mention it, but it's almost half past—

Mrs. Huml. Is it? Goodness! Here I go on gossiping and now I might be late for work! (*Jumps up, finishes her tea standing, runs out by* B. D. *Offstage.*) Are you staying home for lunch?

HUML. Yes.

MRS. HUML. (*Offstage.*) Well, come out here! I'll show you where it is. (*Short pause. Then* HUML *slowly rises and shuffles out by* B. D. *Pause. Offstage.*) It's stew. Leave it in the pot and then just put it on the stove as is. Wait until it's warm, then dish it out and shove the pot back in there—

(MISS BALCAR *and* KRIEBL *enter by* B. D., *carefully carrying Puzuk between them. They are followed by* HUML, *fully dressed and spruced up.* MISS BALCAR *and* KRIEBL *place Puzuk on the table.* KRIEBL *plugs in the cord; all sit down as before;* KRIEBL *fiddles with Puzuk.*)

MISS BALCAR. Hope the mixture in his capillaries didn't freeze up—

KRIEBL. No—his siren wouldn't have worked, would it? We can start—

MISS BALCAR. Splendid! Now, put down— (*Dictating.*) Eduard Huml, 1928—beginning of interview 15:55—first question. (*Calls.*) Silence, please! (KRIEBL, *having typed the data on the keyboard, turns the crank, peers into the eyepiece, and presses a button. The loudspeaker gives out a soft rumbling.* KRIEBL *stares closely at his watch; general suspense. Suddenly* BECK, *in an overcoat, enters by* L. D. *All turn towards him.* KRIEBL *again quickly presses a button and turns the crank. The rumbling stops.* BECK, *paying no attention to anybody, angrily stalks to and fro. Longish pause. All follow his movements with some embarrassment. At last,* MISS BALCAR *produces a small box of chocolates out of her pocket, offering them to* BECK.) Chocolate? (BECK *has noticed* MISS BALCAR'S *gesture, but chooses to ignore it.* MISS BALCAR *waits for a moment, then, embarrassed, replaces the box in her*

pocket. BECK *goes on pacing about. Longish uneasy
pause.* MISS BALCAR *nervously glances at* BECK *a few
times, hesitates, then asks.*) Anything wrong, Mr.
Beck? (BECK *gives* MISS BALCAR *a black look, turns
and exits by* B. D., *slamming it.* HUML *looks questioningly at* MISS BALCAR, *but she quickly turns to*
KRIEBL.) Ready now?

KRIEBL. Ready.

MISS BALCAR. (*Calls.*) Silence, please! (KRIEBL
again turns the crank, presses a button, Puzuk *begins
to rumble. Once more,* KRIEBL *stares closely at his
watch. General suspense. After a while,* Puzuk's *red
light goes on.*) Again red! (KRIEBL *quickly presses a
button and turns the crank. The light goes out and the
rumbling stops. Awkward pause.*) He shouldn't have
stayed so long in the fridge—

KRIEBL. Hasn't been there so long.

MISS BALCAR. Well, what's the matter with him?

KRIEBL. The mixture in his capillaries may have
frozen, that's all. He'll have to get warmed up. (*To*
HUML.) Have you an oven?

HUML. Yes. (KRIEBL *unplugs* Puzuk's *cord and together with* MISS BALCAR *carries* Puzuk *out by* B. D.,
which has meanwhile been opened by HUML. HUML
follows. Pause. Offstage.) In there—second door on the
left.

KRIEBL. (*Offstage.*) Perfect fit!

(*Just then,* HUML *and* BLANKA *enter by* R. D., *both a
bit out of breath.* HUML *holds* BLANKA *by the
hand, leads her to the table and seats her at her
place.* BLANKA *is somewhat excited, straightens
her hair.* HUML *is embarrassed.*)

HUML. I'm sorry—it was just a sudden impulse—
I mean, a sort of joke, really—I'm so sorry, do forgive
me—

BLANKA. Promise me it won't happen again!

HUML. You have my word! (*Short pause.* BLANKA *has calmed down, takes shorthand pad off the table and reads.*)

BLANKA. However, just as the various values man wants to achieve are open to various valuations—

HUML. Ah! Yes— (*Begins to pace thoughtfully to and fro, while dictating to* BLANKA *who takes it down in shorthand.*) to various valuations from various points of view—so is the activity man puts forth in order to achieve those values—full stop. Basically, one can say there exist two kinds of activity—a positive one—for instance, the struggle for justice—and a negative one—for example, scheming—full stop. At the same time, the moving force of every activity is that which might be described as ambition—in the broadest sense of the word—ful stop. Regarding ambition, one must again distinguish between two kinds—dash—I mean colon—

BLANKA. Colon?

HUML. Yes, colon: a healthy ambition and an unhealthy one—full stop. By healthy ambition we understand a really fruitful, profound interest in a definite object—man's natural desire to fulfil himself within the sphere of this interest—full stop. On the other hand, when a desire to use one's resources does not stem from inner motives, but is merely a means towards achieving certain superficial values—such as power, money, publicity, etc.—we talk of unhealthy ambition—full stop. (*Halts, ponders, then turns to* BLANKA.) Listen, Blanka, what do you actually think of me?

BLANKA. Who, me?

HUML. Yes, you—

BLANKA. That you're very well educated, Dr. Huml—

HUML. Do be serious, please!

BLANKA. I'm being serious—

HUML. Naughty little thing, aren't you? (*Looks at*

his watch.) Let's finish at least this paragraph. Where did we stop?

BLANKA. (*Reads.*) But is merely a means towards achieving certain superficial values—such as power, money, publicity, etc.—we talk of unhealthy ambition.

HUML. (*Again begins pacing thoughtfully to and fro, while dictating to* BLANKA.) Whilst positive activity stems above all from healthy ambition, negative activity stems mostly from unhealthy ambition—full stop. Naturally, the above is only a general scheme and as such presupposes some deviations—as for example, when negative activity stems from healthy ambition, or—on the contrary—when unhealthy ambition leads to positive activity—full stop. Got it?

BLANKA. Yes.

HUML. Well, that'll be all for today. Thank you very much.

BLANKA. Pleasure, I'm sure. (*Shoves shorthand pad and pencil into her briefcase which has been lying on the table, closes briefcase, gets up.*)

HUML. Tomorrow at nine again, all right?

BLANKA. Yes, Dr. Huml.

HUML. And don't forget to give that message to Mr. Pittermann—

BLANKA. If I don't get hold of him, I'll leave it with Mrs. Blaha—

HUML. O.K. (BLANKA *just stands, waiting for something.* HUML *is at a loss. Awkward pause.*)

BLANKA. May I have my coat?

HUML. Good gracious! (HUML *runs towards* B. D., *but before he can leave, the doorbell rings.* HUML *halts, turns to* BLANKA.) Would you mind—there—in the wardrobe— (BLANKA *exits by* B. D. HUML *crosses to* R. D., *peers through the peep-hole, then opens.* BLANKA *stands outside the door, wearing a coat and carrying her briefcase.*)

BLANKA. Good morning—

HUML. Good morning, Blanka, do come in—

BLANKA. Am I not too early?

HUML. Not at all, I'm glad you're here already now, I'm expecting someone at twelve, so we'll have to cut it short a bit. May I—

BLANKA. Thanks— (HUML *helps* BLANKA *out of her coat, carries it out by* B. D., *returns at once.* BLANKA *has meanwhile taken a shorthand pad and pencil out of her briefcase. She puts briefcase on table and sits down in her place.*)

HUML. Well, what's the news?

BLANKA. They've mended the lift.

HUML. Finally! And what about the heating, working all right now?

BLANKA. Not yet. And how do you feel, Dr. Huml?

HUML. Thanks, almost back to normal, still a bit shaky, you know, that's all. I've been out already a few times, as a matter of fact, I might drop in at the Institute day after tomorrow— (*Pause.*) Well, ready?

BLANKA. I'm ready—

HUML. O.K. Write down— Chapter Five— Regarding Values— Introduction. (*Begins to pace thoughtfully to and fro, while dictating to* BLANKA, *who takes it down in shorthand.*)

BLANKA. Is that a title?

HUML. Yes. By a value we mean that which satisfies some human need—semicolon—the structure of values thus always reflects the structure of human needs—full stop. We distinguish material values—for example, food, clothes, houses, etc.—from spiritual values—for instance, particular ideas, or pieces of knowledge, relationship to other people, artistic experiences, etc.—full stop. Various people have at various times and in various circumstances various needs— (*Suddenly stops and turns to* BLANKA.) I wonder if you realize what we've forgotten.

BLANKA. Put the kettle on for coffee?

HUML. Correct!

(BLANKA *gets up and exits by* B. D., *leaving it open. At that moment,* RENATA *enters irritably by* L. D., *wearing* MRS. HUML'S *apron.*)

RENATA. The Dolomites! The Dolomites! That's all you can talk to me about!

HUML. Come on, kitty-cat, pull yourself together! (HUML *walks over to* RENATA, *puts his arms lightly around her and begins soothingly to kiss her cheeks, forehead, hair. To start with,* RENATA *resists a little, but gradually gives in. They end up locked in a long, passionate kiss.* RENATA *then gently frees herself— she is smiling now—and throws her arms around* HUML'S *neck.*)

RENATA. You know what I dreamed about last night?

HUML. What?

RENATA. That we got married in a mosque!

HUML. That's absurd—

RENATA. Well, you see, that's the sort of dreams I have! (*Kisses* HUML, *then releases him, takes him by the hand and leads him up the stairs towards the bedroom. She stops at the door and turns to him.*) This is our kiln!

HUML. Our mosque—

(RENATA *kisses* HUML *once more and they both exit by* U. D., *closing the door behind them. Just then,* MISS BALCAR *and* KRIEBL *enter by* B. D., *followed by* HUML. HUML *closes the door, all three slowly cross to the table, sit down as before and wait. Longish uneasy pause.*)

MISS BALCAR. Well he let us know if he gets too hot?

KRIEBL. The siren functions normally— (*Longish uneasy pause. To* HUML.) I've got an aunt in the country.

HUML. Oh?

KRIEBL. I spend my summer holidays with her. It's not in the mountains, but there are lakes—

HUML. How nice— (*Longish uneasy pause.*)

MISS BALCAR. (*To* KRIEBL.) Won't it do him some harm, the way we keep moving him about?

KRIEBL. No—he's used to it, isn't he? (*Longish uneasy pause.*)

HUML. (*To* MISS BALCAR.) I realize that just now asking questions is your job rather than mine—

MISS BALCAR. Go on, you may ask anything you like—

HUML. You said I was the subject of your enquiry—

MISS BALCAR. That's right.

HUML. I'd be interested to know in what sense precisely, I mean—how far—

MISS BALCAR. Completely.

HUML. As I see, there's an anthropological aspect to your work—which means I'll surely find myself on familiar ground! Besides, it's rather logical that you feel you must get to know a person in the round if you want to understand his actions—

MISS BALCAR. Are you familiar with anthropology?

HUML. Well, anthropology is not exactly my field, but I do work in social sciences—

MISS BALCAR. Really? These questions have been ignored here in recent years. Therefore the need to fill in the gap is all the more pressing.

HUML. I believe there are some facts one might be able to lean on; the rest of the world has been dealing with the problem of man for years—

MISS BALCAR. We're aware of that. Particularly the so-called synthetic anthropology, as it has been developed in the United States, is very closely related to our own research. Naturally, we are trying to learn from foreign experiments, even though in principle we don't propose simply accepting their results in a mechanistic way.

HUML. Well, that's clear enough, you have your own specific requirements. And how far do you lean on the results concerning the subject of man arrived at by other scientific disciplines?

MISS BALCAR. We lean on them a great deal, but actually only in sort of negative way. You see, for the various specialized sciences, man represents no more than a particular function or a general category—be it as a highly developed mammal, as a maker, or as a psychological prototype—and thus in each case their concept of man depicts no more than one particular, partial characteristic—which is moreover always shared by many other individuals as well. On the other hand, we are concerned with the man in the round, a man whose complexity has not been simplified, whose human uniqueness has been preserved. This means working on a qualitatively new level where we cannot get by with a simple accumulation of what is already here—rather, on the contrary, we must start at the point where the individual specialized sciences end.

HUML. Well, this is indeed a modern approach to the subject! What's more, your results might have a really broad application. If, for example, you managed to find a way to shape human individuality scientifically, it would be of the greatest importance not only to yourselves, but to the whole of society—

MISS BALCAR. Most certainly! If nothing else, it might open a way to a rationally organized limiting of such phenomena as, for example, alienation.

(*Suddenly,* BECK, *in his overcoat, enters by* B. D. *He takes no notice of anybody, angrily crosses to the Upstage wall, halts, turning back on the others. All watch him with some embarrassment. After a while he speaks up without turning.*)

BECK. Tomorrow I'm going fishing and that's that! (*Awkward pause.*)

MISS BALCAR. Surely, you don't mean that, Mr. Beck! What would we do without you? You do know how much we need you— (*Awkward pause. BECK does not react.*) But who would direct our whole research work? Not one of us has anywhere near your qualifications— (*Awkward pause. BECK does not react.*) Really, you couldn't do that to us, Mr. Beck— (*Awkward pause. Suddenly BECK turns and snaps.*)

BECK. You heard me! (BECK *stalks energetically out by* L. D. *and slams it.* HUML *looks questioningly at* MISS BALCAR, *but she quickly turns to* KRIEBL.)

MISS BALCAR. Do you know where Mrs. Huml works?

KRIEBL. Where?

MISS BALCAR. In a toy shop!

KRIEBL. (*To* HUML.) Oh? (*Just then, Puzuk's sharp siren starts wailing Offstage.*) What did I tell you! Now he's hot!

(MISS BALCAR *and* KRIEBL *jump up and run out by* B. D. HUML *follows. All of a sudden, the telephone starts ringing and goes on for quite a while. At last,* HUML *runs in by* U. D., *wearing only his trousers and shirt, with a towel around his neck. He reaches the telephone and picks up the receiver.*)

HUML. (*Into the telephone.*) Yes, speaking. (*Pause.*) Is it absolutely necessary? You see, I've been ill—may I ask who's calling? (*Pause.*) I see— I see— I'll be here—not at all— (*Slowly replaces the receiver, ponders for a moment, then shakes his head in puzzlement and slowly returns upstairs. Shortly after,* MISS BALCAR *and* KRIEBL *enter by* B. D., *carefully carrying Puzuk between them. They are followed by* HUML, *fully dressed and spruced up.* MISS BALCAR *and* KRIEBL *place Puzuk on the table.* KRIEBL *plugs in the cord; all sit down as before;* KRIEBL *fiddles with Puzuk.*)

Miss Balcar. Hope his insulators haven't burned out—

Kriebl. No—there'd be smoke coming out of him, wouldn't there? We can start—

Miss Balcar. Splendid! Now, put down— (*Dictating.*) Eduard Huml, 1928—beginning of interview 16:32—first question. (*Calls.*) Silence, please! (Kriebl, *having typed the data on the keyboard, turns the crank, peers into the eyepiece, and presses a button. The loudspeaker gives out a soft rumbling. Kriebl stares closely at his watch; general suspense. After a while, Puzuk's green light goes on.*) Splendid! It's green!

Kriebl. About time! (*Out of Puzuk's loudspeaker issues an effeminate voice.*)

Puzuk. Tell me— (*Pause. Suspense.*) Tell me— (*Pause. Suspense.*) Tell me please— (*Pause. Suspense.*) Karel?

Kriebl. (*To Puzuk.*) What is it?

Puzuk. May I have a little rest?

END OF ACT ONE

ACT TWO

HUML's *Flat: The same as in Act One. Again the Stage is empty. Offstage the sound of water filling up a receptacle. When, judging by the sound, the receptacle is full, the sound ceases and* HUML, *wearing a suit, enters by* B. D., *with a small watering-can full of water. He slowly crosses to the cactus on the commode Upstage and begins to water it with care. Then, sound of key turning in* R. D. *and* MRS. HUML *enters, wearing an overcoat, carrying a bulging shopping bag and under her arm a table-lamp.*

HUML. Hello!

MRS. HUML. Hello! Well?

HUML. (*Finishes watering, puts can behind commode, walks over to* MRS. HUML *and takes lamp from her.*) Let me see——

MRS. HUML. (*Puts bag on table and exhausted sinks into a chair.*) Did you talk to her?

HUML. Handy, isn't it? How much.

MRS. HUML. Hundred and fifty.

HUML. Not bad—— (*Lamp in hand, exits by* L. D. *Offstage.*) I'd better put in a stronger bulb—— (*Pause. Returns by* L. D., *having left lamp in the study and having taken off his jacket. He is putting on his dressing-gown over his shirt; closes door.*) Have we a stronger bulb? (*Short pause.*)

MRS. HUML. You are a horrible man!

HUML. What's the matter?

MRS. HUML. It would be too much for you to say one kind word to me!

HUML. Well, thank you very much, you found a wonderful lamp—— (*Pause.*) I'm awfully pleased with it—— (*Pause.*) It's nice that you're home again——

27

MRS. HUML. Oh, skip it!

HUML. Well, what do you want, for heaven's sake? (*Notices a newspaper sticking out of the shopping bag, pulls it out, crosses to easy-chair, sits down, makes himself comfortable and begins to glance through the paper. Pause.*)

MRS. HUML. I asked a question—

HUML. (*Without looking up.*) So did I—

MRS. HUML. Why don't you look for yourself! You know where we keep the bulbs— (*Pause.* HUML *is reading.*) You never kiss *me* on the neck!

HUML. (*Looks up, surprised.*) What did you say?

MRS. HUML. I said, you never kiss me on the neck—

HUML. I've kissed you enough during my lifetime!

MRS. HUML. But not on the neck, with me that never excited you! Make no mistake, we women remember that sort of thing very well!

HUML. Should you stop speaking for womankind and see about starting dinner? (*Again turns to his paper.*)

MRS. HUML. (*Gapes at him for a while, then gets up excitedly, grabs her shopping bag off the table.*) I'm a fool, I really am! (MRS. HUML, *offended, walks out by* B. D. HUML *looks after her, for a moment remains sitting, then slowly gets up and with the paper open in his hands shuffles towards* B. D. *He halts at the threshold and speaks towards Backstage.*)

HUML. Vlasta, dear— (*Pause.*) You know I didn't mean it that way— (*Pause.*) Remember the Alps? In that old mill? (*Pause, then* MRS. HUML *returns by* B. D., *tying an apron over her dress.*)

MRS. HUML. The Alps! The Alps! That's all you can talk to me about!

HUML. Come on, kitty-cat, pull yourself together! (HUML *approaches* MRS. HUML, *puts his hands on her shoulders from behind, pulls her towards himself and gives her a long kiss on her neck.* MRS. HUML *half-*

closes her eyes and smiles happily. Then gently feels herself.)

Mrs. Huml. You see! I need so little to be happy—

Huml. I had no idea it meant so much to you—

Mrs. Huml. What would you like for dinner? There's cauliflower, or sausages—or I could make you an omelette, if you like—

Huml. Sausages would be just fine—

Mrs. Huml. And during dinner you'll tell me how it went! I can hardly wait—

(Mrs. Huml *hastens out by* b. d. Huml *stands for a while, pondering, newspaper in hand, then shuffles up the stairs to the bedroom and exits by* u. d. *Just then,* Blanka *enters by* b. d., *carefully carrying small tray with two cups of coffee. She puts it on the table, sits down in her place, takes a cup and stirs.* Huml *enters by* b. d., *fully dressed, carrying small bowl with biscuits, leaves door ajar, crosses to table and offers* Blanka *a biscuit.* Blanka *takes one.)*

Blanka. Thank you—

Huml. (*Puts bowl on table, sits down, stirring his coffee. Longish pause.*) Are you going to see Pitter-mann today?

Blanka. If I can get hold of him—

Huml. Well, if you do see him, please tell him to send me—perhaps via you—his comments on the editorial plan, I'd like to have another look at them—

Blanka. I'll tell him— (*Pause. Both sip their coffee.*) We can go on working—

Huml. Why don't you finish your coffee—

Blanka. No, really—

Huml. All right? Well, where did we stop?

Blanka. (*Takes shorthand pad and pencil from table and reads.*) To agree on a particular definition of happiness which would be satisfactory for all.

HUML. Ah, yes! Now—new paragraph. When one particular need of a man has been satisfied—it actually ceases thereby—full stop. However, man is —to coin a phrase—in constant need of further needs —for the moving force of his life is not that state in which all his needs have been satisfied, but the process of continually satisfying them—man's effort towards their gratification—full stop. (HUML *gets up and begins to pace thoughtfully to and fro, while slowly dictating to* BLANKA. *Now and then he halts at table and takes a sip of coffee.* BLANKA. *takes down his dictation in shorthand and she too occasionally takes a sip of her coffee.*) There exist situations—for example in some advanced western countries—in which all the basic human needs have been satisfied and still people are not happy—they experience feelings of depression, boredom, frustration, etc.—full stop. In these situations man begins to desire that which in fact he perhaps does not need at all—he simply persuades himself he has certain needs which he does not have— or he vaguely desires something which he cannot specify and thus cannot strive for—full stop. Hence, as soon as man has satisfied one need—i.e. achieved happiness—another so far unsatisfied need is born in him, so that every happiness is always simultaneously a negation of happiness, because— (HUML *halts near* BLANKA *and stares at her.* BLANKA *does not realize what goes on, thinking he is merely searching for a precise formulation. Longish pause. Suddenly,* HUML *leaps towards* BLANKA, *falls on his knees, grabs her shoulders and tries to kiss her.* BLANKA *is startled and cries out.*)

BLANKA. Oh! (*A short struggle ensues,* HUML *attempting to put his arms around* BLANKA *and kiss her,* BLANKA *resists, finally she gives him a push,* HUML *loses his balance and falls down.* BLANKA *jumps up.*) You should be ashamed of yourself, Dr. Huml! (BLANKA, *alarmed, runs out by* R. D., HUML *looks sheepishly after her for a moment, then quickly gets up and follows her out by* R. D. *From behind the door his receding voice is heard.)*

HUML. (*Calling Offstage.*) Blanka! Blanka! Blanka —listen to me!

RENATA. (*Offstage.*) Does she ever dust in here?

HUML. (*He enters by* B. D., *crosses to table, sits down.*) I'm sure she does— (*Shortly after* HUML, RENATA *enters by* B. D., *she is puting on* MRS. HUML's *dressing-gown over her dress.*)

RENATA. Don't I remind you of her?

HUML. A bit—

RENATA. And you don't mind?

HUML. I do—

(RENATA *takes off the dressing-gown, takes it out by* B. D., *returns at once, closes the door, crosses to the easy-chair, sits down, lights a cigarette. Short pause.*)

RENATA. And what do you say to her when she asks if you love her?

HUML. When possible, I try to change the subject. What about some lunch, kitty-cat? There's some stew—

RENATA. Listen, Eddi—

HUML. Mmnn—

RENATA. Promise me you'll finally wind it up in some reasonably way! We just can't go on like this! It makes me suffer more than you think. Most of all in the evenings when we're together, driving around in your car, having fun, kissing each other—and all the time I know that in a while it'll be all over, you'll go back to her, to the warm family hearth, where meanwhile she's been mending your socks or your underpants; she'll give you a bite to eat, she'll bring your pajamas, you'll turn on the radio softly and then you'll both climb into one huge bed and stay there the whole night— (*Pause.*) I'm sure you'll think I'm being silly, but do you know what bothers me most at those moments?

HUML. What?

RENATA. The idea that you'll be sleeping with her after you go home—

HUML. You know very well that I now sleep with her only very rarely—

RENATA. I hope you aren't making it all up just to calm me down! Does it ever occur to you what it's like for me, always having to keep secrets, to hide, to pretend in front of others that I don't know you, having to come to you like a thief! If it's not worth your while to break it off on my account, you ought to do it for your own sake—just look at yourself! Can't you see the way you're slipping?

HUML. I told you, didn't I, I want to do it in stages. What about some lunch?

RENATA. I know your blessed stages, so far you haven't budged!

HUML. What do you mean? Only this morning I began to prepare the ground.

RENATA. Did you? How? Did you tell her you love me?

HUML. For a start, I said I find you sexually exciting.

RENATA. Well that's at least something. What did she say?

HUML. She insisted I should part with you. What about some lunch?

RENATA. I hope you didn't promise her any such thing!

HUML. She was so insistent, I had to agree—on the surface. But deep down I kept my own counsel and I didn't commit myself to anything definite.

RENATA. Really? And then? Did you suggest to her you want a divorce?

HUML. I said you were rather counting on it—

prospectively. What about some lunch? There's some stew—

RENATA. I'll have a look—— (RENATA *gets up and exits by* B. D. HUML *slowly follows her. At the door he meets* RENATA, *who has just returned, wearing a coat.* HUML *turns and walks with her towards* R. D.) Well, can I count on you discussing it with her this evening?

HUML. And what if she asks me why I didn't tell her before, right when I started with you?

RENATA. Just tell her you're very sorry, but for a long time you saw it as only a passing affair—not really worth mentioning——

HUML. But that's exactly what she minds most about the whole thing——

RENATA. Don't worry, you'll find a way! (*The doorbell rings.* HUML *starts.*)

HUML. They're here! (*Grabs* RENATA *and drags her back to* B. D.) Wait in the bathroom, I'll fetch you in a minute—— (HUML *pushes* RENATA *out by* B. D., *and hastens to* R. D., *first peers through the peep-hole, then opens.* MISS BALCAR *enters first.* KRIEBL *and* MACHAL *follow, each carrying two vast suitcases;* BECK *is the last to enter. All wear overcoats.*)

MISS BALCAR. Dr. Huml?

HUML. Yes. Come in——

MISS BALCAR. We phoned——

HUML. Yes, I've been expecting you——

MISS BALCAR. This is Mr. Kriebl, our technician; Mr. Machal, our surveyor; I'm Dr. Balcar—and this is Mr. Beck, our supervisor——

HUML. How do you do——

MISS BALCAR. The boys will have to unpack their instruments and set them up——

HUML. Instruments?

MISS BALCAR. That's right. Where can they go so they won't be too much in our way?

HUML. Well, perhaps there—to the study—— (KRIEBL *and* MACHAL, *carrying their suitcases, exit by* L. D. HUML *crosses to* MISS BALCAR.) Allow me——

MISS BALCAR. Thank you— (HUML *helps* MISS BALCAR *out of her coat and turns to* BECK.)

HUML. Won't you take off your coat?

(BECK *makes a disparaging gesture.* HUML, *puzzled, takes* MISS BALCAR'S *coat out by* L. D. *and instantly returns.* MISS BALCAR *makes herself comfortable in the easy-chair,* HUML *offers a chair to* BECK *who does not react, but instead begins to stalk thoughtfully to and fro, still in his overcoat.* HUML *uneasily sits down. Short pause.*)

MISS BALCAR. I'm so glad you've agreed to spare us some of your time—

HUML. It's my duty, isn't it?

MISS BALCAR. Most people don't quite see our work that way—

HUML. They're governed by all sorts of prejudices, I suppose—

MISS BALCAR. I'm afraid so. (*Short awkward pause.* MISS BALCAR *glances nervously at* BECK *who is still pacing around, hesitates for a moment, then produces a small box of chocolates out of her pocket, offering them to* BECK.) Chocolate? (BECK *has noticed* MISS BALCAR'S *gesture, but chooses to ignore it.* MISS BALCAR *waits for a moment, then, embarrassed, replaces the box in her pocket. Pause.*)

HUML. May I ask what are the instruments you've brought with you?

MISS BALCAR. Apart from a variety of measuring equipment, it's mainly Puzuk.

HUML. Puzuk?

MISS BALCAR. We call him that. It's a small automatic calculator, model CA-213, suitably adapted to our particular needs, of course.

HUML. I had no idea you were so modernized— (*Short awkward pause.* MISS BALCAR *again nervously glances at the pacing* BECK, *hesitates, then asks.*)

MISS BALCAR. Anything wrong, Mr. Beck? (BECK

gives Miss Balcar *a black look, turns and exits by*
L. D., *slamming it.* Huml *looks questioningly at* Miss
Balcar, *but she quickly turns to him.*) Is your wife
out?

Huml. Yes. She has a job.

Miss Balcar. Oh? Where?

Huml. She's the manager of a toy shop.

Miss Balcar. Is she really? How nice! When I need
any toys I'll get in touch with her.

Huml. But of course! She'll be delighted to help
you. Have you children?

Miss Balcar. No.

(*Short pause. Then* Machal, *wearing a lab-coat,
enters by* L. D., *a pencil stuck behind his ear. He
takes no notice of anybody, slowly climbs the
stairs, halts outside the bedroom, pulls a plumb-
line from his pocket and lowers it all the way to
the floor, taking care the string remains free of
the stairs. After the plumb-line has settled, he
hoists it and replaces it in his pocket, produces
a grubby slip of paper on which he scribbles some
notes. Then he exits by* U. D. *Short pause.*)

Huml. It's the bedroom—up there—

Miss Balcar. That's right.

Huml. I'm sorry, but—

Miss Balcar. Yes?

Huml. You didn't make quite clear on the telephone—

Miss Balcar. We purposely provide beforehand only
the vaguest information. You see, people might prepare themselves, and that would affect the authenticity
of their testimony.

Huml. Ah! Yes—I see—

Miss Balcar. Wait a minute— (*Listens concen-
tratedly. From Offstage a sort of faint rumbling. Calls
towards* L. D.) Mr. Kriebl?

KRIEBL. (*Offstage.*) What is it?

MISS BALCAR. Why does he rumble?

KRIEBL. (*Offstage.*) Doesn't want to say. Got a bit cold in the suitcase, I suppose—

MISS BALCAR. But he always gets sweaty in the suitcase—

KRIEBL. (*Offstage.*) We've got a new case.

MISS BALCAR. You'll let me know when you're ready, won't you?

KRIEBL. Won't be long— (*Short pause.*)

HUML. You're carrying somebody around in a suitcase?

MISS BALCAR. (*Smiles.*) Of course not. We're talking about Puzuk. He's very sensitive, you know. It's always hard to make him feel acclimatized. Yet, his condition is terribly important to us. When he feels right, our work literally flies along. On the other hand, when he's being difficult it makes a lot of complications for us. The most sensitive thing about him are the little relays. Their performance is affected even by the weather—pressure, temperature, humidity—all influence them. When it's raining, or when there's fog we prefer to stay away from fieldwork altogether— (*Just then* L. D. *opens and* KRIEBL, *in his lab-coat, appears.*)

KRIEBL. We can start—

MISS BALCAR. Splendid! (MISS BALCAR *quickly gets up and exits with* KRIEBL *by* L. D. *As soon as they are gone,* HUML *jumps up, runs to* B. D., *opens it and softly calls.*)

HUML. Renata—

RENATA. (*Offstage, softly.*) Took you ages—

HUML. Get ready— (HUML *leaves* B. D. *open and swiftly exits by* L. D. *which he carefully leaves ajar.*)

MRS. HUML. (*Offstage.*) Wait until it's warm, then dish it out and shove the pot back in there. Have some bread with it; there's beer in the fridge—

HUML. (*Offstage.*) Shall I leave some for you?

(MRS. HUML *hastily enters by* B. D., *wearing her dress and carrying a make-up case.*)

MRS. HUML. Finish it if you like. I'll get something for dinner— (HUML *ambles in by* B. D., *dressed in his pajamas, dishevelled, with* MRS. HUML's *coat over one arm, in the other hand her shopping bag.* MRS. HUML *crosses to the mirror, spreads the contents of her case on the commode and hastily puts on her lipstick, mascara and powder, and combs her hair.* HUML *stands nearby with her coat and bag and waits. Pause.*) And did you suggest to her you want to part with her?

HUML. I said you were rather counting on it— prospectively—

MRS. HUML. You really said that? And then?

HUML. What d'you mean, "then?"

MRS. HUML. I mean, how did you go on preparing the ground?

HUML. Well, I didn't laugh at a whole lot of her jokes, for example, and altogether I was more reserved—

MRS. HUML. You're not just trying to jolly me along, are you?

HUML. Not in the least. I want to put an end to it, I really do. Only you've got to try and understand it's not an easy matter. We've been having an affair for over a year, she has nobody but me, she can't imagine her life without me, she promises herself a lot from our relationship—she rather counts—prospectively— on my divorcing you and marrying her—well, you know how it is, women are terribly sensitive about these things; in any case, it's going to be a blow for her.

MRS. HUML. I've never even suggested you shouldn't do it tactfully, that goes without saying, doesn't it?

HUML. And what do I say if she asks me why I didn't tell her right away, before she began to really count on me?

MRS. HUML. Just tell her you're very sorry, but it was a misunderstanding, that you saw it as only a passing affair.

HUML. But that's exactly what she keeps suspecting—

MRS. HUML. Don't worry, you'll find a way! (*Pause. Mrs. HUML is combing her hair.*)

HUML. Listen, Vlasta—

MRS. HUML. Yes?

HUML. You wouldn't like to settle the whole thing with her yourself, would you? After all, you're not so deeply involved in this relationship—

MRS. HUML. For heaven's sake, what would that look like! Nonsense! You have a word with her today and that's that! (*Finishes her make-up, cleans her comb, swiftly throws all her make-up things into the case.*) Dictating today?

HUML. Yes.

MRS. HUML. Scripts?

HUML. No, that thing for the V.C.A. (*MRS. HUML shoves the make-up case into her shopping bag, held by HUML, who then helps her into her coat.*)

MRS. HUML. Shall I buy that table-lamp for you?

HUML. Would you?

(*MRS. HUML is dressed, takes her shopping bag from HUML, surveys herself in the mirror, makes sure her keys are in the bag, then crosses to R. D., accompanied by HUML. At the door she halts and turns towards HUML.*)

MRS. HUML. Well, bye—and I'm keeping my fingers crossed for you! (*Offers HUML her cheek, he kisses it.*)

HUML. Bye— (*MRS. HUML exits, HUML shuts the door, stretches, looks at his watch, then leisurely shuffles out by B. D., leaving it open. Offstage HUML's singing is heard, interrupted by sounds of his washing: splashing of water, sighing, brushing of teeth, etc.*

After a while, sounds suddenly stop. R. D. *opens and* HUML *and* BLANKA, *both out of breath, enter.* HUML *is fully dressed and spruced up. He holds* BLANKA *by the hand, leads her to the table, seats her at her place.* BLANKA *is somewhat excited, straightens her hair.* HUML *is embarrassed.*) I'm sorry—it was just a sudden impulse—I mean, a sort of joke, really—I'm so sorry —do forgive me—

BLANKA. Promise me it won't happen again!

HUML. You have my word! (*Short pause.* BLANKA *has calmed down, takes shorthand pad from table and reads.*)

BLANKA. So that every kind of happiness is always simultaneously a negation of happiness, because—

HUML. Ah, yes! Now—new paragraph—

BLANKA. Shall I cross out "because?"

HUML. Do. (*Begins to pace thoughtfully to and fro, while slowly dictating to* BLANKA, *who takes it down in shorthand.*) Happiness is thus—on the one hand— in the exact meaning of the term—something very unstable, transient, mutable—on the other hand, however, it is also—as a general state—something very permanent—because man always desires to be happy —it is, therefore, a sort of ideal—towards which human activity rises again and again—an ideal which, however, can never in fact be fully attained by man —full stop. Therefore, happiness is not something given once and for all—we keep losing it and we keep having to strive for it again and again—full stop. (*Halts, ponders, then turns to* BLANKA.) Blanka—

BLANKA. Yes, Dr. Huml?

HUML. What sort of memories have you of your childhood?

BLANKA. Nice ones—

HUML. So have I. My childhood is forever bound up with the countryside where I grew up and with the people around me.

BLANKA. So is mine—

HUML. I still carry it all inside me—the Rapid River, the elms above the dam, which we used to climb as boys so many times—Black Pond in which old Vavra drowned his wife—the pine-trees, the firs, and all that flint under foot, the purple prunus and the juniper—gossamer, after the fields had been ploughed —old Danek, whose cow rolled over and smothered his goat one Easter—Rosie, the miller's daughter, who could make such marvellous mouth music—the little chapel at the crossroads, all those melancholy autumn walks through the oak woods right under the Castle— anyway, all this means nothing to you, nothing at all— (*Pause. He is still dreaming.*)

BLANKA. Well, shall we go on? You said you were short of time—

HUML. (*Does not respond, but watches* BLANKA *for a moment, then asks.*) Are you a virgin?

BLANKA. What?

HUML. I said, are you a virgin?

BLANKA. I beg your pardon!

HUML. It's kindly meant, I ask as your friend—

BLANKA. No, I'm not.

HUML. That's what I thought! Well—let's go on. Where did we stop?

BLANKA. (*Reads.*) Therefore, happiness is not something given once and for all—we keep losing it and we keep having to strive for it again and again.

HUML. (*Once more starts thoughtfully pacing and dictating.*) Particularly in the present world—distinguished by the gigantic development of communications—the attainment of happiness is becoming an increasingly difficult task—full stop. Man's effort to achieve satisfaction of his needs—that is, to attain specific values—directly or indirectly characterizes all human activity—full stop. Yet, as the different values man wants to attain can be viewed from different angles—brackets—for example, from the angle of the observer's individual scale of values, or from a broader

angle, i.e. that of a particular period—end of brackets
—sorry, how did it go before the brackets?

BLANKA. (*Reads.*) Yet, as the different values man
wants to attain can be viewed from different angles—

HUML. Cross out what's inside the brackets—

BLANKA. All of it?

HUML. All of it. (HUML *halts near* BLANKA *and
stares at her.* BLANKA *does not realize what goes on,
thinking he is merely searching for a precise formulation. Longish pause. Suddenly,* HUML *leaps towards*
BLANKA, *falls on his knees, grabs her shoulders and
tries to kiss her.* BLANKA *is startled and cries out.*)

BLANKA. Oh! (*A short struggle ensues,* HUML *attempting to put his arms around* BLANKA *and kiss her,*
BLANKA *resists, finally she gives him a push,* HUML
loses his balance and falls down. BLANKA *jumps up.*)
You should be ashamed of yourself, Dr. Huml!
(BLANKA, *alarmed, runs out by* R. D., HUML *looks
sheepishly after her for a moment, then quickly gets
up and follows her out by* R. D. *from behind the door
his receding voice is heard.*)

HUML. (*Calling Offstage.*) Blanka! Blanka! Blanka
—listen to me!

(*Short pause.* U. D. *slowly opens and* HUML *appears in
the bedroom door, shirt opened at the neck, tie
loose, jacket in his hand. He stretches a bit and
leisurely descends the stairs, while puttting on his
jacket, buttoning his shirt and straightening his
tie. After him* RENATA *appears in the door,
slightly dishevelled, zipping up her dress. She
too walks down, crosses to the mirror and tidies
herself in front of it, ignoring him, who stands
silently, sheepishly, nearby. When she finishes at
the mirror,* RENATA *crosses to the easy-chair, sits
down and lights a cigarette. She seems distant
and avoids looking at* HUML, *who watches her
and is beginning to get slightly nervous. Longish
uneasy pause.*)

RENATA. You're just overworked, that's all!

HUML. Mmnn— (*Longish uneasy pause.*)

RENATA. About time something happened!

HUML. Mmnn— (*Longish uneasy pause.*)

RENATA. What you need is to get away from it all. Physical work. Change of diet. Fresh air. What does she actually give you for dinner?

HUML. Well—all sorts of things—sausages—omelettes—

RENATA. Do you ever eat any carrots?

HUML. Not really—

RENATA. No—this way it'll never work!

(*Pause.* HUML *surreptitiously glances at his watch, crosses to table, picks up the things left over from lunch and from his coffee with* BLANKA *on tray, carries it to* B. D., *puts it on the commode, opens the door, takes tray out, returns at once, shuts door and remains standing by the commode, watching* RENATA *rather unhappily.* RENATA *ignores him and goes on smoking.*)

HUML. Listen, Renata—

RENATA. Yes?

HUML. You wouldn't like to settle the whole thing with her yourself, would you? After all, you're not so deeply involved in this relationship—

RENATA. For heaven's sake, what would that look like! Nonsense! You have a word with her today, and that's that! (*Longish uneasy pause.*)

HUML. (*Becoming more nervous, again surreptitiously glances at his watch.*) Listen, Renata—

RENATA. Yes?

HUML. I'm expecting some chaps—

RENATA. Who?

HUML. Don't know, they rang me up, they didn't want to say on the phone what it's all about, but it appears to be rather important, most likely they're from—you know—

RENATA. You think so?

HUML. I'd rather they didn't meet you here—

RENATA. In other words, you're throwing me out! May I at least finish my cigarette?

HUML. I mean it for your own sake, too— (RENATA *extinguishes her cigarette, gets up and coldly exits by* B. D., *leaving it open.* HUML *is visibly relieved, crosses to* R. D. *and peers out through the peep-hole.*)

RENATA. (*Offstage.*) Where's my coat?

HUML. Just outside the door— (*Starts towards* B. D. HUML *stops at the mirror and hastily tidies himself up. Just then, the doorbell rings. He rushes to* R. D., *peers through the peep-hole and opens.* RENATA *stands outside, weaing her coat.*)

RENATA. Give us a kiss! (HUML *kisses* RENATA'S *cheek.*) Well?

BLANKA. (*Wearing her coat, enters by* B. D.) Good morning—

HUML. Let me introduce—Miss Blanka, our secretary—Renata, my sister-in-law— (RENATA *and* BLANKA *shake hands, short awkward pause, then* BLANKA *takes her briefcase from the table and crosses to* R. D. *To* BLANKA.) Well, again many thanks for your patience—your co-operation—your punctuality—

BLANKA. Quite all right. Good bye—

HUML. Good bye—

RENATA. Good bye— (HUML *opens* R. D. *for* BLANKA, *she exits,* HUML *walks over to* RENATA.) What was that?

HUML. She takes my dictation—

RENATA. Let's hope so! Well?

HUML. Won't you take off your coat?

RENATA. Failed again, I bet.

HUML. Couldn't help it.

RENATA. Why?

HUML. The circumstances weren't right. She was a bit irritable and in rather a hurry to get to work. Won't you take off your coat?

RENATA. Another opportunity missed! (RENATA *takes off her coat, helped by* HUML, *who then slowly recedes towards* B. D., *followed by* RENATA.)

HUML. Look, it's not the last time I'm going to see her, I'll give it another try this evening—

RENATA. Evening! Evening! Again another evening! Listen, be honest, aren't you perhaps postponing the whole thing on purpose?

HUML. Why on earth should I do that? (*Disappears with the coat by* B. D.)

RENATA. Maybe you actually still love her—

HUML. (*Offstage.*) You know very well I stopped loving her long ago! I just like her as a friend, a housewife, a companion of my life—

RENATA. (*Has meanwhile followed* HUML *out by* B. D. *Offstage.*) Some housewife! Does she ever dust in here?

(MISS BALCAR *and* KRIEBL *enter by* B. D., *carefully carrying* PUZUK *between them. They are followed by* HUML. MISS BALCAR *and* KRIEBL *place* PUZUK *on the table.* KRIEBL *plugs in the cord; all sit down as before;* KRIEBL *fiddles with* PUZUK.)

MISS BALCAR. Hope his insulators haven't burned out—

KRIEBL. No—there'd be smoke coming out of him, wouldn't there? We can start—

MISS BALCAR. Splendid! Now, put down— (*Dictating.*) Edward Huml, 1928—beginning of interview 16:32—first question. (*Calls.*) Silence, please! (KRIEBL, *having typed the data on the keyboard, turns the crank, peers into the eyepiece, and presses a button. The loudspeaker gives out a soft rumbling.* KRIEBL *stares closely at his watch; general suspense. After a while,* PUZUK'S *green light goes on.*) Splendid! It's green!

KRIEBL. About time!

(*Out of* PUZUK'S *loudspeaker issues an effeminate voice.*)

PUZUK. Tell me— (*Pause. Suspense.*) Tell me— (*Pause. Suspense.*) Tell me please— (*Pause. Suspence.*) Karel?

KRIEBL. (*To* PUZUK.) What is it?

PUZUK. May I have a little rest?

KRIEBL. But you haven't done a stroke of work yet!

PUZUK. I got so tired from all this moving about—

KRIEBL. All right, go on then, for all I care— (KRIEBL *quickly presses a button and turns the crank. The light goes out.*)

MISS BALCAR. Doesn't seem to be feeling very well today, does he?

KRIEBL. Just showing off, that's all.

MISS BALCAR. (*To* HUML.) Sometimes he's like a child—

KRIEBL. The other day, he was just as awkward, I got a bit tired of it, so I simply shoved him into the garage for a couple of hours, turned off the light and made him solve several hundred differential equations. You should have seen him afterwards—he was killing himself to please me! It's a question of unbringing, too, you know!

MISS BALCAR. That's what I say—like a child— (*Longish uneasy pause.*)

KRIEBL. (*To* HUML.) I wouldn't mind buying some of those high altitude plums for the children—

HUML. Take as many as you like—free, of course— I wouldn't hear of taking money for them—

KRIEBL. Well, if I may—thanks— (*Longish uneasy pause.*)

HUML. (*To* MISS BALCAR.) I'm sorry to keep bothering you with questions—

MISS BALCAR. Goodness no, it's a pleasure to discuss our work with you—

HUML. You do understand, don't you, it's sort of professional interest on my part—in a way—

MISS BALCAR. I quite understand. After all, we're really colleagues—so to speak—

HUML. Precisely. I'd be interested to know more about the exact procedure you use in shaping human personality—

MISS BALCAR. Well, we proceed from the following, altogether logical, proposition: if men are related by the general aspects of their personalities, they must necessarily, on the other hand, be differentiated by those aspects which are particular and random. In other words, the gravitational focus of human individuality does not lie in any aspects which can be established as predictable, but, on the contrary, in those which defy all laws, all norms, and thus constitute precisely the vast and neglected sphere of coincidence.

HUML. It sounds convincing. But how can one cope with this sphere—scientifically, I mean.

MISS BALCAR. That's exactly where Puzuk plays such an important part. He simply compares the quantum of all the possible relationships from among all the pieces of information about a particular individual which we've fed into him, or which he has acquired on his own—he compares these concurrently with the laws and norms of all the scientific disciplines previously fed into his memory—in order to eliminate all those relationships which an existing scientific discipline can establish as predictable. Simultaneously, he rejects those elements which he'd already encountered with other individuals and which, therefore, could be considered potentially predictable. Thus he gradually arrives at a certain comprehensive structure of maximally radom relationships—and in fact this is already—basically—a sort of condensed model of human individuality.

HUML. How very original! Indeed, both the theory

and the practical application— I must say— (*Just then,* L. D. *opens and* MACHAL *appears, in his lab-coat, pencil behind his ear. All turn towards him.*)

KRIEBL. (*To* MACHAL.) What's the matter?

MACHAL. Have you seen the safety bolt of the moisture meter?

KRIEBL. You usually keep it in your sandwich bag.

MACHAL. It's not there.

KRIEBL. I don't know, then— (MACHAL *stands about for a while, emptily staring ahead, then slowly turns and starts out, as* KRIEBL *addresses him.*) Emil—

(MACHAL *stops short at the door, turns towards* KRIEBL, *who quickly gets up, crosses to* MACHAL, *whispers to him some instructions, while pointing towards* B. D., MACHAL *nods, understands, agrees.* KRIEBL *pats his head in a friendly manner,* MACHAL *dodges at once, apparently cannot tolerate this sort of endearment.* KRIEBL *returns to his place,* MACHAL *exits by* L. D., *leaving it open, instantly returns, carrying a string-bag, again leaves* L. D. *open, ambles towards* B. D., *paying no attention to anybody.*)

MISS BALCAR. (*To* MACHAL.) Have you weighed the bedclothes yet?

MACHAL. (*Halts at* B. D., *standing with his back to the room, after a moment grumbles.*) What?

MISS BALCAR. I said, have you weighed the bedclothes yet?

MACHAL. (*Without turning.*) I'm measuring the moisture of the walls—

MISS BALCAR. I see—

MACHAL. (*Short pause, still facing the door, grumbles.*) All this fuss and bother— (*Exits by* B. D. *Short pause.*)

HUML. (*To* MISS BALCAR.) Do you mind my asking just one more question—how do you select your sub-

jects— I mean—today, for example, why did you call
on me of all people, why not somebody else?

Miss Balcar. Entirely superficial reasons—

Huml. Oh? Such as?

Miss Balcar. We called on you—same way we
called on many others—simply because your name
begins with an H, and your house has an odd number.

Huml. I'm afraid, I'm not responsible for my name,
nor for the number of my house! Matter of pure coincidence, isn't it?

Miss Balcar. The more random the key to our
selection of samples, the more representative the sample—depending on it's size, that is—

Huml. So, as far as you're concerned, I represent
nothing but a random sample here, is that it?

Miss Balcar. That's right.

Huml. I see—

Miss Balcar. We can't help proceeding this way in
the first stage. I'm afraid, we haven't been able to call
on everybody so far— (*Just then,* Michel *enters by*
b. d., *carrying the string-bag full of plums.* Kriebl
winks at him, exuding agreement and thanks. Michel,
paying no attention to anybody, shuffles out by l. d.
Pause. To Kriebl.) Shall we have another try?

Kriebl. Why not—

Miss Balcar. (*Calls.*) Silence, please!

(Kriebl *turns the crank, presses a button,* Puzuk
begins to rumble. Kriebl *stares closely at his*
watch; general suspense. Suddenly, Beck *in his*
overcoat enters by l. d. *All turn towards him.*
Kriebl *again quickly presses a button and turns*
the crank. The rumbling stops. Beck, *ignoring*
everybody, angrily stalks Upstage and plants
himself there facing the wall, his back to the
room. All watch him with some embarrassment.
After a while, he speaks up without turning.)

BECK. Tomorrow I'm going fishing and that's that! (*Awkward pause.*)

MISS BALCAR. Surely, you don't mean that, Mr. Beck! What would we do without you? You do know how much we need you— (*Awkward pause.* BECK *does not react.*) But who would direct our whole research work? Not one of us has anywhere near your qualifications— (*Awkward pause.* BECK *does not react.*) Really, you couldn't do that to us, Mr. Beck— (*Awkward pause. Suddenly* BECK *turns and snaps.*)

BECK. You heard me! (BECK *stalks energetically out by* R. D. *and slams it.* HUML *looks questioningly at* MISS BALCAR, *but she quickly turns to* KRIEBL.)

MISS BALCAR. Ready now?

KRIEBL. Ready.

MISS BALCAR. (*Calls.*) Silence, please!

(KRIEBL *again turns the crank, presses a button,* PUZUK *begins to rumble. Once more,* KRIEBL *stares closely at his watch; general suspense. Suddenly,* L. D. *opens and* MACHAL *reappears, wearing earphones, they are connected to an instrument he carries in his arms. All turn towards him.* KRIEBL *again quickly presses a button and turns the crank. The rumbling stops.* MACHAL *shuffles to the Right wall, pulling out of his pocket a funnel, connected to the instrument by a flexible tube, presses the funnel against the wall and listens with great concentration to whatever goes on inside his earphones. Pause.*)

KRIEBL. (*To* MACHAL.) Did you find the safety bolt of the moisture meter? (*Pause.* MACHEL *does not respond, removes the funnel from the wall, lets it drop, so that it hangs on its tube; produces from his pocket a grubby slip of paper on which he laboriously notes the measurements; then crosses to the back wall, presses the funnel against it and again listens. Rais-*

ing his voice somewhat.) Did you find the safety
bolt of the moisture meter? (MACHAL *does not respond, removes the funnel from the wall, let's it
drop down, makes another entry; then crosses to the
Left wall, presses the funnel against it and again
listens. Raising his voice still more.*) I say, Emil, did
you find the safety bolt of the moisture meter? (*Pause.
MACHAL does not respond, removes the funnel from
the wall, lets it drop down, and makes an entry.*)

MISS BALCAR. He can't hear you—

KRIEBL. I suppose not— (MACHAL, *having finished,
slowly crosses to* KRIEBL *and hands him the slip of
paper.*) Thanks, Emil— (KRIEBL *smooths out the slip
of paper on the table, then slides it into* PUZUK.
MACHAL, *carrying the instrument and trailing the
funnel, ascends towards the bedroom. On the stairs he
trips over the tube, falls down, for a while does not
move, then slowly gets up, grumbles, mounts the stairs,
stumbles on the last step, exits by* U. D. *Short pause.*)

MISS BALCAR. Ready now?

KRIEBL. Ready.

MISS BALCAR. (*Calls.*) Silence, please! (KRIEBL *once
more turns the crank, presses a button,* PUZUK *begins
to rumble.* KRIEBL *stares closely at his watch. General
suspense. After a while,* PUZUK's *red light goes on.*)
Again red! (*Just then, the red light goes out and the
green light goes on.*) No—it's green!

KRIEBL. About time!

(*Out of* PUZUK's *loudspeaker issues an effeminate
    voice. There is a short pause after each question.*
    PUZUK's *red and green lights alternately keep
    flashing on and off.*)

PUZUK. Which is your favourite tunnel? Are you
fond of musical instruments? How many times a year
do you air the square? Where did you bury the dog?
Why didn't you pass it on? When did you lose the

claim? Wherein lies the nucleus? Do you know where you're going and do you know who's going with you? Do you piss in public, or just now and then? (*Short pause. PUZUK's loudspeaker emits only a soft rumbling. HUML gets up energetically.*)

HUML. What's the meaning of this? (HUML *bangs the table and angrily stalks towards* B. D. *Just as he reaches it, the door is flung open, disclosing* BLANKA.)

BLANKA. You should be ashamed of yourself, Dr. Huml! (BLANKA *slams the door shut.* HUML *for a moment freezes in astonishment, then swiftly turns and crosses to* R. D. *Just as he reaches it, the door is flung open, disclosing* MACHAL.)

MACHAL. Have you seen the safety bolt of the moisture meter? (MACHAL *slams the door shut.* HUML *for a moment freezes in astonishment, then swiftly turns and crosses to* L. D. *Just as he reaches it, the door is flung open, disclosing* RENATA.)

RENATA. Do you ever eat any carrots? (RENATA *slams the door shut.* HUML *for a moment freezes in astonishment, then swiftly turns and runs up towards the bedroom. Just as he reaches* U. D., *the door is flung open, disclosing* BECK.)

BECK. Tomorrow I'm going fishing and that's that! (BECK *slams the door shut.* HUML *for a moment freezes in astonishment, then swiftly turns and runs down again to* B. D. *Just as he reaches it, the door is flung open, disclosing* MRS. HUML.)

MRS. HUML. You're not just trying to jolly me along, are you? (MRS. HUML *slams the door shut.* HUML *for a moment freezes in astonishment, then swiftly turns and runs to the table.*)

KRIEBL. Give me your high altitude plums!

MISS BALCAR. Dr. Huml?

PUZUK. Which is your favourite tunnel? How many times a year do you air the square? Why didn't you pass it on? Wherein lies the nucleus? Do you piss in public, or just now and then? (HUML *runs over to* L. D., *in which* BLANKA *appears.*)

BLANKA. Have you seen the safety bolt of the moisture meter? (BLANKA *disappears,* HUML *rushes up to* U. D., *in which* MACHAL *appears.*)

MACHAL. You should be ashamed of yourself, Dr. Huml! (MACHAL *disappears,* HUML *rushes down to* B. D., *in which* RENATA *appears.*)

RENATA. Do you ever eat any jolly plums? (RENATA *disappears,* HUML *runs to* R. D., *in which* BECK *appears.*)

BECK. Tomorrow I'm going carroting and that's that! (BECK *disappears,* HUML *runs to* L. D., *in which* MRS. HUML *appears.*)

MRS. HUML. You're not just trying to jolly along the fish, are you? (MRS. HUML *disappears,* HUML *runs back to the table.*)

KRIEBL. Dr. Huml? (HUML *turns to* MISS BALCAR, *who gets up.*)

MISS BALCAR. Give me your high altitude plums!

(*Suddenly, all the characters appear on the Stage. All, including* KRIEBL *and* MISS BALCAR, *begin variously to criss-cross from one door to another, while repeating, together with* PUZUK, *over and over their questions and demands, addressed to* HUML. *Their movements and speech become faster and faster, their voices louder, so that the end impressions of this Scene is an ever-increasing acoustic and visual chaos.* HUML *keeps desperately rushing among them, as though seeking some sort of haven.*)

MRS. HUML. You're not just trying to jolly along the fish, are you? You're not just trying to jolly along the fish, are you? (*Etc.*)

BECK. Tomorrow I'm going carroting and that's that! Tomorrow I'm going carroting and that's that! (*Etc.*)

RENATA. Do you ever eat any jolly plums? Do you ever eat any jolly plums? (*Etc.*)

MACHAL. You should be ashamed of yourself, Dr. Huml! You should be ashamed of yourself, Dr. Huml! (*Etc.*)

BLANKA. Have you seen the safety bolt of the moisture meter? Have you seen the safety bolt of the moisture meter? (*Etc.*)

KRIEBL. Dr. Huml? Dr. Huml? (*Etc.*)

MISS BALCAR. Give me your high altitude plums! Give me your high altitude plums! (*Etc.*)

PUZUK. Which is your favourite tunnel? Are you fond of musical instruments? (*Etc.*)

(*When the uproar becomes intolerable,* PUZUK *emits his well-known siren-type wail. At once, the tumult ends;* KRIEBL, MISS BALCAR *and* HUML *resume their places at the table, all the other characters instantly disappear.*)

HUML. What's the meaning of this?

MISS BALCAR. (*To* KRIEBL.) Switch him off! (KRIEBL *presses a button and turns the crank. The lights which have been flashing until now go out, the rumbling stops.* HUML *sits down again. Awkward pause.*) That's all we needed! (*To* KRIEBL.) A short, I suppose, wasn't it?

KRIEBL. Shouldn't think so. More likely a stray electric impulse.

MISS BALCAR. Blast! (*To* HUML.) Those are the so-called stray thoughts—at such moments he's quite unaware of what's happening inside him. (*To* KRIEBL.) From the start I had a notion he wasn't somehow feeling all right today! Are you going to try and locate that damn impulse?

KRIEBL. I'd like to, but I can't—the union, you know. But I'll see a chap I know in the workshop, he'll fix it for me in a jiffy—for a bottle of booze, that is. (MACHAL *enters by* U. D., *all turn towards him, he pays no attention to them, slowly descends, while re-*

moving the earphones from his ears, still carrying the *instrument with the funnel.)* Emil—

MACHAL. What is it?

KRIEBL. We'll be packing up now— (MACHAL *carries* *the instrument out by* L. D., *leaving it open, returns* *and together with* KRIEBL, *who has meanwhile un-* *plugged the cord, carries out* PUZUK *by* L. D. *Pause.)*

MISS BALCAR. I'm so sorry we've troubled you for nothing today. May we drop in again after the week-end? (*Pause.* HUML *stares quizzically at* MISS BALCAR.)

HUML. Listen, where do you work, actually?

MISS BALCAR. Well, formally, we're attached to the Institute of Sociology, we even use their premises, but in fact we are a more-or-less independent research group.

HUML. Oh, I see—

MISS BALCAR. Why do you ask?

HUML. No special reason—

MISS BALCAR. (*Pause.*) May we come after the weekend? (*Pause.*) Dr. Huml— (*Pause.*) May we come back after the weekend?

HUML. What?

MISS BALCAR. I wondered—may we trouble you once more—when Puzuk is all right again—

HUML. I'm sorry, but I think it'd be no use—

MISS BALCAR. Why? I mean, to us it'd be of great use!

HUML. I'm afraid, it wouldn't—not even to you.

MISS BALCAR. I don't follow you!

HUML. Look, I've no doubt you mean well, I respect the enthusiasm with which you've committed yourself to this project, but as a man who has devoted many years to professional work in the social sciences—try as I may—I can't take the whole matter seriously—

MISS BALCAR. What do you mean?

HUML. I mean I can't take the whole matter seriously.

MISS BALCAR. But why?

HUML. What I've just seen, as well as what you've told me about your work, has been quite enough to convince me that from the point of view of science the whole project is nothing but an unfortunate mistake. And I hope you'll see that my conscience as a scientist wouldn't allow me to co-operate on a project which I'm absolutely sure is thoroughly mistaken.

MISS BALCAR. But you talked quite differently before—

HUML. That was a little misunderstanding—

MISS BALCAR. Besides, such a sweeping statement would have to be substantiated!

HUML. Nothing easier, if you really care to know. For example, it should be enough to point out the rather obvious fact that things which from one angle appear as predictable, may from another angle appear as coincidental, and *vice versa;* because predictability and coincidence are no absolute categories, nor are they any objectively existing and differentiated spheres of reality—their extent depends merely on the chosen viewpoint, or angle. It can't be helped, from the scientific point of view everything is always to some extent predictable, while science itself is but a gradual disclosing of this predictability; what we call coincidental is either that which lies beyond the radius of predictability, or simply that which so far we've been unable to establish as predictable. In other words, your endeavour to isolate the element of coincidence and use it as a means of shaping human individuality bears no relationship to science whatsoever. Moreover, it is bound to miss its goal completely. Why? Because it replaces reality—i.e. an objective totality—with a chimera of one of its specific relative and wholly subjective aspects. Science is able merely to keep reaching up towards the totality of a unique personality. It can do this within the limits of that which —at a given moment—it is capable of illuminating and describing as predictable. It can never reach beyond these limits, because man, as an objective totality, fundamentally contains the dimensions of infinity. And I'm afraid the key to a real knowledge of the human individual does not lie in some greater or lesser understanding of the complexity of man as an object of scientific knowledge. The only key lies in man's complexity as a subject of human togetherness, because the limitlessness of our own human nature is so far the only thing capable of approaching—however imperfectly—the limitlessness of others. In other words, the personal, human, unique relationship which arises between two individuals is so far the only thing that can—at least to some extent—mutually unveil the secret of those two individuals. Such values as love, friendship, compassion, sympathy and the unique and irreplaceable mutual understanding—or even mutual conflict—are the only tools which this human approach has at its disposal. By any other means we may perhaps be able more or less to explain man, but we shall never understand him—not even a little—and therefore we shall never arrive at a basic knowledge of him. Hence, the fundamental key to man does not lie in his brain, but in his heart. (MISS BALCAR *begins to cry softly. Surprised.*) Why are you crying? (MISS BALCAR *goes on crying.* HUML *is baffled. Pause.*) I didn't mean to hurt you— (MISS BALCAR *goes on crying. Pause.*) It was just my private opinion— (MISS BALCAR *goes on crying. Pause.*) It never occured to me you'd take it personally— (MISS BALCAR *loudly sobs,* HUML *watches her for a moment in some embarrassment, then he quickly approaches her, takes her gently in his arms and begins to stroke her hair.* MISS BALCAR *does not resist, on the contrary—still crying—she rests her head on* HUML's *chest.*) Just forget everything I said!

MISS BALCAR. It's my whole life—

Huml. I'm sure I was wrong—perhaps I didn't quite understand your explanation—

Miss Balcar. (*Tearfully.*) It's all I have in the whole world!

Huml. I do apologize, I'm sincerely sorry—

Miss Balcar. (*Crying.*) You've humiliated me terribly! How bad and malicious you all are! You don't understand anything—anything at all—

Huml. Calm yourself, please—

Miss Balcar. How I hate you for what you've done to me! (Huml, *still stroking* Miss Balcar's *hair, begins to kiss her gently on her tearful eyes, cheeks, lips, and on her hair.*)

Huml. (*Whispers.*) There, there, don't cry— I was being cruel—cynical— I'm ashamed of myself— (Miss Balcar *presses herself closer to* Huml, *still loudly sobbing. There follows prolonged, passionate kissing.* Kriebl *and* Machal *enter by* L. D., *both dressed in their overcoats, and carrying the large suit-cases.* Kriebl *also carries the string-bag full of plums.* Miss Balcar *and* Huml *jump apart. Embarrassment.*)

Miss Balcar. Well, many thanks—thank you—both of you. See you tomorrow then. Good bye!

Kriebl. Good bye—

Machal. Good bye—

(Kriebl *and* Machal *exit by* R. D., Huml *hesitantly walks out by* B. D., *instantly returns, carrying* Miss Balcar's *coat, helps her to put it on.* Miss Balcar *buttons it up and pulls it straight; crosses to* Huml, *throws her arms around his neck and gently covers his face with kisses; then she strokes his hair and starts towards* R. D. Huml *stands in the middle of the room, rather nonplussed.* Miss Balcar *opens the door, stops at the threshold and turns to* Huml.)

Miss Balcar. May I ring you up tomorrow?

Huml. (*Surprised.*) Yes—of course—

MISS BALCAR. Will you have some time for me?

HUML. Certainly——

MISS BALCAR. Say something nice to me before I go!

HUML. Kitty-cat——

MISS BALCAR. I don't like that——

HUML. Dearest——

MISS BALCAR. That's a bit better——

HUML. Darling—— (MISS BALCAR *runs over to* HUML, *gives him a kiss, runs back, smiling happily, stops at the door and again turns.*)

MISS BALCAR. My name's Anna——

HUML. Well——bye, Anna——

MISS BALCAR. Bye, Eddi! (MISS BALCAR *exits by* R. D., *closing it.* HUML *stares after her for a while in utter bewilderment, then shakes his head, sighs deeply, looks at his watch, looks around the room, ambles to the commode, reaches behind it, pulls out a small watering-can and shuffles out by* B. D. *Offstage, sound of water filling up a receptacle. When, judging by the sound, the receptacle is full, the sound ceases, and* MRS. HUML *enters by* B. D. *She is wearing an apron over her dress, and carries a tray with dinner for two: plates, sausages, mustard, two glasses, a bottle of wine, a basket with bread, knives and forks. Setting the table, she calls towards the bedroom.*)

MRS. HUML. Dinner! (*When she has finished the table,* MRS. HUML *pours some wine into the glasses, sits down and begins to eat, while* U. D. *opens and* HUML *enters, wearing a dressing-gown over his shirt and trousers. He is slightly dishevelled, obviously having just had a nap, leisurely descends, sits down opposite* MRS. HUML, *spreads a napkin in his lap and also starts eating. Longish silence is finally interrupted by* MRS. HUML.) Well?

END OF PLAY

M/F duo   p11-12   Huml + Renata
                     ↳ see p22 also

M/F duo p15/16 Huml + Mrs H,

F mono p15/16 Mrs H,

M/F Duo   p19/20 Huml / Blanka

M/F Duo p20/21   Huml / Blanka

M/F Duo (ctd) p22 Huml /Renat
                  → see p. 11/12

ACT TWO

M/F Duo p27/28   Huml + Mrs H.

M/F Duo p31/32 Huml / Renata

M/F Duo p33-35 Huml / Ms Balcar

M/F Duo p37/38 Huml /mrs H.

M   Mono p55/56   - Dr Huml/